Winter
Wonderland

ISBN 0-590-46657-7

Copyright © 1934 (Revised) WB Music Corp. Used by permission.
Illustrations copyright © 1993 by Jacqueline Rogers.
All rights reserved. Published by Scholastic Inc.
by arrangement with Warner Bros. Publications Inc.
CARTWHEEL BOOKS is a registered trademark of Scholastic Inc.

12 11 10   2/0

Printed in the U.S.A.   24

First Scholastic printing, October 1993

Winter Wonderland

Words by Dick Smith
Music by Felix Bernard

Illustrated by Jacqueline Rogers

Cartwheel
·B·O·O·K·S·®

SCHOLASTIC INC.
New York Toronto London Auckland Sydney

Sleigh-bells ring,
are you listening?

In the lane,
snow is glistening,

A beautiful sight,
we're happy tonight,

Walking in a Winter Wonderland!

Gone away is the bluebird,
here to stay is a new bird;

He sings a new song,
as we go along,

Walking in a Winter Wonderland!

In the meadow we can build a snowman,
Then pretend that he is Parson Brown;

He'll say, "Are you married?"
We'll say, "No, man!

But you can do the job when you're in town!"

Later on, we'll conspire,
As we dream by the fire,

To face unafraid,
the plans that we made,

Walking in a Winter Wonderland!

In the meadow we can build a snowman,
And pretend that he's a circus clown;

We'll have lots of fun with Mr. Snowman,

Until the other kiddies knock him down!

When it snows,
it's so thrilling,

Tho' your nose, gets a chilling.

We'll frolic and play

the Eskimo way,

Walking in a Winter Wonderland!

Winter Wonderland

Words by Dick Smith ◇ Music by Felix Bernard